Dear Parents:
Your child's love of reading starts here!

Every child learns to read in a different way and at his or her own speed. Some go back and forth between reading levels and read favorite books again and again. Others read through each level in order. You can help your young reader improve and become more confident by encouraging his or her own interests and abilities. From books your child reads with you to the first books he or she reads alone, there are I Can Read Books for every stage of reading:

SHARED READING
Basic language, word repetition, and whimsical illustrations, ideal for sharing with your emergent reader

BEGINNING READING
Short sentences, familiar words, and simple concepts for children eager to read on their own

READING WITH HELP
Engaging stories, longer sentences, and language play for developing readers

READING ALONE
Complex plots, challenging vocabulary, and high-interest topics for the independent reader

ADVANCED READING
Short paragraphs, chapters, and exciting themes for the perfect bridge to chapter books

I Can Read Books have introduced children to the joy of reading since 1957. Featuring award-winning authors and illustrators and a fabulous cast of beloved characters, I Can Read Books set the standard for beginning readers.

A lifetime of discovery begins with the magical words **"I Can Read!"**

Visit www.icanread.com for information
on enriching your child's reading experience.

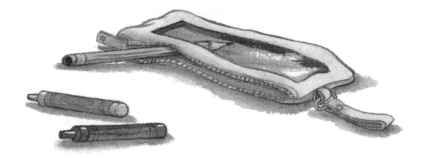

JUN 0 3 2019

I Can Read!

SHARED
My First
READING

Biscuit
Goes to School

story by ALYSSA SATIN CAPUCILLI

pictures by PAT SCHORIES

HarperCollins*Publishers*

Biscuit Goes to School Text copyright © 2002 by Alyssa Satin Capucilli Illustrations copyright © 2002 by Pat Schories All rights reserved. No part of this book may be used or reproduced in any manner whatsoever without written permission except in the case of brief quotations embodied in critical articles and reviews. Manufactured in U.S.A. For information address HarperCollins Children's Books, a division of HarperCollins Publishers, 195 Broadway, New York, NY 10007. www.harpercollinschildrens.com

Library of Congress Cataloging-in-Publication Data

Capucilli, Alyssa.
  Biscuit goes to school / story by Alyssa Satin Capucilli ; pictures by Pat Schories.
    p. cm.—(A my first I can read book)
  Summary: A dog follows the bus to school, where he meets the teacher and takes part in the activities of the class.
  ISBN-10: 0-06-028682-2 (trade bdg.) — ISBN-13: 978-0-06-028682-8 (trade bdg.)
  ISBN-10: 0-06-028683-0 (lib. bdg.) — ISBN-13: 978-0-06-028683-5 (lib. bdg.)
  ISBN-10: 0-06-443616-0 (pbk.) — ISBN-13: 978-0-06-443616-8 (pbk.)
  [1. Dogs—Fiction. 2. Schools—Fiction.] I. Schories, Pat, ill. II. Title. III. Series.
PZ7.C179Bisf 2002   00-049881
[E]—dc21   CIP
                                                        AC

❖

18 19 20 LSCC 60 59 58 57

*For the wonderful students, teachers,
librarians, and parents who have
welcomed Biscuit into their schools!*

Here comes the school bus!
Woof, woof!

Stay here, Biscuit.

Dogs don't go to school.

Woof!

Where is Biscuit going?

Is Biscuit going to the pond?

Woof!

Is Biscuit going to the park?
Woof!

Biscuit is going to school!
Woof, woof!

Biscuit wants to play ball.
Woof, woof!

Biscuit wants
to hear a story.
Woof, woof!
Shhh!

Biscuit wants a snack.

Woof, woof!

Oh, Biscuit!

What are you doing here?

Dogs don't go to school!

Oh, no!

Here comes the teacher!

Woof!

Biscuit wants

to meet the teacher.

Woof!

Biscuit wants
to meet the class.
Woof, woof!

Biscuit likes school!

Woof, woof!

And everyone at school
likes Biscuit!
Woof!

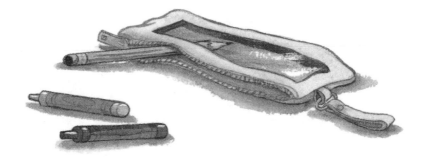